Tell me A STORY

Emily Bannister

illustrated by Barbara Chotiner

Kane Miller
A DIVISION OF EDC PUBLISHING

Tell me a story to BRIGHTEN my day.
Send me a story with the things
you want to say.

Send me a story
down a RIVER or SEA.
Send me a story
to bring you CLOSER to me.

Send me a story
about **traveling** so far.
Send me a story
about just who **you** are.

Send me a story
about long, long ago.
Send me a story
of mountains and snow.

Send me a story whatever the weather.

Send me a story;
we belong together.

Send me a story
of all the things that you've seen!

Send me a story
about tea with the Queen.

Send me a story
from HiGH up in the clouds.
Send me a story
from DOWN among the crowds.

Send me a story
to SHARE late at night.
Send me a story
where I CUDDLE you tight.

But of all of these *letters* and words that you scrawl, it's the STORY of *YOU* that's the best of them all.

So write of ADVENTURES and JOURNEYS you take,
AND please SHARE with me, WHATEVER you make.

To start with...

You'll need an idea,
a place or a thing.
Something to talk of or even to sing.
There should be a start,
a middle and end.
It could be about you
and maybe a friend.
Describe what you see,
and how it may feel,
make it exciting but also seem real.